The Adventures of

FAT

THE
RATROD

FATTY

Written by Mitch Oxborough and Anne Winter.
Illustrated by John Horvath and coloured by Glo Hill

The Adventures of Fatty the Rat Rod

Author: © Mitch Oxborough & Anne Winter

National Library of Australia Cataloguing-in-Publication entry

Author:	Oxborough, Mitch; Winter, Anne
Title:	Fatty the rat rod : the adventures of Fatty the rat rod / Mitch Oxborough and Anne Winter.
ISBN:	9780987462503 (hbk.)
Target Audience:	For primary school age.
Dewey Number:	A823.4

Published with the assistance of InHouse Publishing.

For Our Kids
Grace - Anne, Lyndon & Darcy

Fatty was a farm truck, built in 1951.

She was sitting in the paddock,

thinking all her work was done.

Some forty years of toiling hard had left her tired and beat,
and now her paint was fading in the rain and sun and heat.

The grass grew tall around her,
her left guard all pushed in,
and though her nose was dented,
she'd kept her cheeky grin.

The farmer didn't need her now because she was too old.

He'd gone and bought a brand new truck,

which was big and loud and bold.

The new truck laughed at Fatty.

He said, 'Your work is done,

and it's time for you to stand aside,

for now I'm number one.'

She knew this was her only chance

to tell him a thing or two,

For she had been the number one

when she'd arrived, brand new.

Up before the sun each day,
        not home till after dark,
with pigs or cows or fencing gear,
        she'd really left her mark.

Fatty never missed a beat,

and she'd never missed a day.

There was the time she'd swum the creek

to take the cows their hay.

And when she helped to fight the fire
that nearly took the town,
the water tank was on her back
while the firemen hosed it down.

She said, 'You may be bright and shiny,

all eager, loud and bold.

But there will come a day, my friend,

when you, too, will be old.'

'There will be another one to take your place, it's true,

And maybe you will say to him as I now say to you;'

'Off you go now, do your chores,

　　　　　for my working days are done,

and I've earned this little quiet time,

　　　　　　just dozing in the sun.'

So Fatty sat and rested for there was nothing else to do.

But as the years passed slowly by,

she grew very sad and blue.

She wished that she could work again
and to help with every chore.
She was tired of sitting around all day;
it was really such a bore.

But little did our Fatty know,

that soon would come the day,

when she'd be sold at auction and taken far away.

She was towed off to the Scrap Yard

and this made her very scared.

It was busy, it was noisy and it seemed that no-one cared.

She watched as all the other cars
were crushed up and were scrapped.
She feared it would be her turn next
and she felt that she was trapped.

So she thought if she stayed quiet,
    they might forget that she was there,
and perhaps, if they forgot her,
    from the scrap pile she'd be spared.

Now huddled in the corner,
    behind some bins of steel,
She wished for one who'd care for her;
    how sad it made her feel.

Then one day a phone call came,

an excited man did say;

'We'd like to buy the old farm truck.

We'll come get her right away!'

So, Fatty's wish was granted.

        She couldn't believe her luck.

Her new owners brought a trailer,

        behind a big white truck.

The man put his hand on Fatty's guard
and gave her a gentle smile.
'It's ok Girl, we're here now.
We'll be home in just a while.'

Now, Fatty was feeling happy.

 The sun made her old chrome glow.

With the help of a forklift to push her up,

 she was secured and ready to tow.

She sat up on the trailer with a smile across her face.

And so began the journey home to Fatty's brand new place.

Halfway there it started, pounding down with rain.
It washed her clean of dust and grime,
                                    'til Fatty shone again.

The trip was long and tiring,
    but she enjoyed her newfound luck,
With dented cheeks both glowing red from
    the tail lights on the truck.

When they arrived at her new home,

      she was pushed into the shed.

'We'll fix you up; you'll see, old girl,'

      her new owner smiled and said.

He cleaned her chrome and polished her paint,

but he didn't remove the rust.

'Fatty, I think we'll leave it there.

In me, you'll have to trust.'

Though Fatty was soon all shined and buffed,
                she still looked far from new.
Mixed with her green paint were bumps and dents,
                with rust marks showing through.
'We will be saving other cars,
            and it's you who will bring them home.
For that, my dear, you'll need more power,
                not fancy paint and chrome.'

Fatty couldn't help but notice the big smile upon
his face, as he carefully removed her engine and
swung the new one into place.
'This will give you what you need,
    but we'll have to fix your brakes.
        Fatty, I'll get you running well
            and I'll do whatever it takes.'

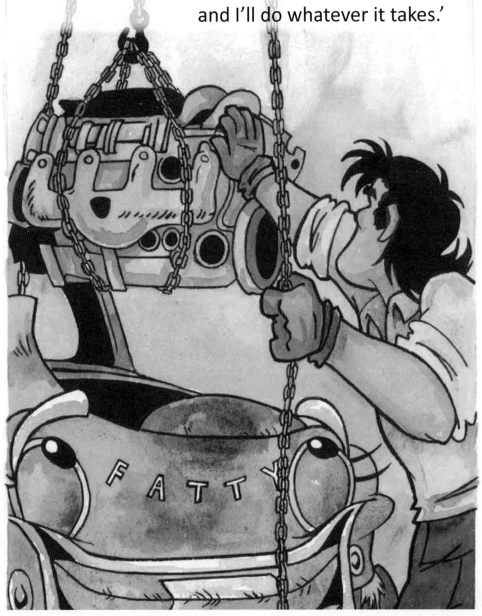

Soon Fatty sat on six new tyres.

Her springs were low and firm.

Those brand new brakes would stop her fast

and she had new shocks for the turns.

Her new headlights did shine so bright,

the windscreen clean and clear,

and Fatty laughed, 'Well, look at that!

I can see both far and near!'

'You'll need a good strong towbar
and a solid timber tray,
We'll build it new from something old,
cause that's the Rat Rod way.'

So he bent the steel and cut the wood
then screwed it all down tight.
Stepping back to admire his work,
said; 'Fatty, that looks just right.'

Then at last, came the day,

     when all the work was done.

It was time to fire the old girl up,

     to see how she would run.

Everyone crowded all around,

     watching Fatty eagerly.

With fingers crossed and breath held tight,

     her owner turned the key.

A small puff of soot burst from her pipes,
    as Fatty leapt into life.
Loudly, her engine rumbled and revved,
    amidst the cheers of delight.

Oh, such a sweet note, a wonderful sound!
    Fatty was running once more.
It'd been many years since the throb of an engine
    had rattled the glass in her doors.

'Fatty, my dear, you're ready now,
and we have a big surprise.
The Hot Rod Show has come to town,
you won't believe your eyes.'

Never had she seen before, a sight to rival this.
All paint and chrome and happy smiles,
to Fatty, it was bliss.

Hot Rod cars were everywhere
and Fatty felt quite shy.
But she realised that was silly,
and here's the reason why...

They loved her dents and scratches,
          her engine big and loud,
and when Fatty drove around the town,
          she'd never felt so proud.

The fancy rods were all so nice.
          They didn't run her down.
Just 'cause her paint – once shiny green
          – was marked with rusty brown.

As Fatty drove with her new friends,
she heard an up-tempo beat.
The rock and roll music filled her soul
as they rumbled down the street.

She saw big hair and sideburns
and girls in frilly skirts,
and ponytails and bobby socks
and multi-coloured shirts.

Lots of children gathered 'round,
 some even climbed inside her.
Their parents snapping photographs,
 and chatting with Fatty's owner.

A giggling child with sticky hands
gave her rusty paint a pat,
and then he honked on Fatty's horn,
as behind her wheel he sat.

Fatty's big heart was filled with joy;
she loved the Hot Rod Show.
Yet, she was now proudly a rescue truck,
all set to make her first tow.

No longer wasting in the field,

Fatty's tough and strong once more.

She may be rusty and a little banged up,

but she's young at heart, for sure.

Now, Fatty is a Rat Rod.

Her farming days are done.

Yes, Fatty is a Rat Rod,

and her days are filled with fun.

THE RATROD

www.fattytheratrod.com

 Fatty The Rat Rod

In a paddock, beneath a tree,
beside a burnt-out shed.
Her sad eyes hold a story,
but the words remain unsaid.

Then one day...

Printed in Great Britain
by Amazon

86126432R00031